W9-AXV-774

Song of the Flowers

Takayo Noda

Dial Books for Young Readers

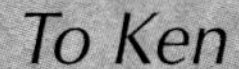

To Ken

My heartfelt thanks to Lauri Hornik and Nancy Leo-Kelly
for giving me their wonderful support and
professional guidance on this project

DIAL BOOKS FOR YOUNG READERS
A division of Penguin Young Readers Group
Published by The Penguin Group
Penguin Group (USA) Inc., 375 Hudson Street, New York, NY 10014, U.S.A.

Penguin Group (Canada), 90 Eglinton Avenue East, Suite 700, Toronto, Ontario, Canada M4P 2Y3
(a division of Pearson Penguin Canada Inc.)
Penguin Books Ltd, 80 Strand, London WC2R 0RL, England
Penguin Ireland, 25 St. Stephen's Green, Dublin 2, Ireland (a division of Penguin Books Ltd)
Penguin Group (Australia), 250 Camberwell Road, Camberwell, Victoria 3124, Australia
(a division of Pearson Australia Group Pty Ltd)
Penguin Books India Pvt Ltd, 11 Community Centre, Panchsheel Park, New Delhi - 110 017, India
Penguin Group (NZ), Cnr Airborne and Rosedale Roads, Albany, Auckland 1310, New Zealand
(a division of Pearson New Zealand Ltd)
Penguin Books (South Africa) (Pty) Ltd, 24 Sturdee Avenue, Rosebank, Johannesburg 2196, South Africa
Penguin Books Ltd, Registered Offices: 80 Strand, London WC2R 0RL, England

 • Designed by Nancy R. Leo-Kelly
Text set in Optima • Manufactured in China on acid-free paper
1 3 5 7 9 10 8 6 4 2

Library of Congress Cataloging-in-Publication Data
Noda, Takayo.
Song of the flowers / Takayo Noda.
p. cm.
ISBN 0-8037-2934-0
1. Flowers—Juvenile poetry. 2. Children's poetry, American.
3. Lullabies, American. I. Title.
PS3564.O285S66 2006 811'.6—dc22 2004028221

The collage artwork for this book was prepared using watercolor paint on
Dieu Donné handmade paper and Fabriano hot- and cold-press paper.

The buttercup asked the dragonfly,
"Will you sing a lullaby
To lull me oh-so-soft to sleep tonight?"
"Why, yes dear," said the dragonfly,
Resting on the clean white fence,
"I'll sing you soft a lullaby
And teach you to fly high within your dreams."

The tulip asked the puffy cloud,
"Will you sing a lullaby
To lull me oh-so-soft to sleep tonight?"
"Why, yes dear," said the puffy cloud,
Floating in the clear blue sky,
"I'll sing you soft a lullaby
And wrap you light and tenderly tonight."

The daisy asked the ladybug,
"Will you sing a lullaby
To lull me oh-so-soft to sleep tonight?"
"Why, yes dear," said the ladybug,
Climbing up the daisy's stem,
"I'll sing you soft a lullaby
And lie beside you as you sleep tonight."

The poppy asked the gentle stream,
"Will you sing a lullaby
To lull me oh-so-soft to sleep tonight?"
"Why, yes dear," said the gentle stream,
With fish deep in her water,
"I'll sing you soft a lullaby
And take you to the ocean in your dreams."

The crocus asked the butterfly,
"Will you sing a lullaby
To lull me oh-so-soft to sleep tonight?"
"Why, yes dear," said the butterfly,
Flitting from flower to flower,
"I'll sing you soft a lullaby
And fan you with my yellow wings tonight."

The pansy asked the rainbow bright,
"Will you sing a lullaby
To lull me oh-so-soft to sleep tonight?"
"Why, yes dear," said the rainbow bright,
Spreading warmth across the sky,
"I'll sing you soft a lullaby
And paint you bands of color in your dreams."

The sunflower asked the honeybee,
"Will you sing a lullaby
To lull me oh-so-soft to sleep tonight?"
"Why, yes dear," said the honeybee,
While making honey busily,
"I'll sing you soft a lullaby
And bring you to my honeycomb in your dreams."

The dandelion asked the shooting star,
"Will you sing a lullaby
To lull me oh-so-soft to sleep tonight?"
"Why, yes dear," said the shooting star,
Flashing in the sky above,
"I'll sing you soft a lullaby
And shower you with stardust in your dreams."

The rose asked the firefly,
"Will you sing a lullaby
To lull me oh-so-soft to sleep tonight?"
"Why, yes dear," said the firefly,
Showing off his magic glow,
"I'll sing you soft a lullaby
And dim my light so you can sleep tonight."

The daffodil asked the crescent moon,
"Will you sing a lullaby
To lull me oh-so-soft to sleep tonight?"
"Why, yes dear," said the crescent moon,
Shining down on everything,
"I'll sing you soft a lullaby
And watch you as you rest your eyes tonight."

The flowers asked the whole wide world,
"Should we sing a lullaby
To lull the children soft to sleep tonight?"
"Yes, certainly," said everyone,
Nodding oh-so-joyfully,
"Let's sing them soft a lullaby
And wish them only happy dreams tonight."